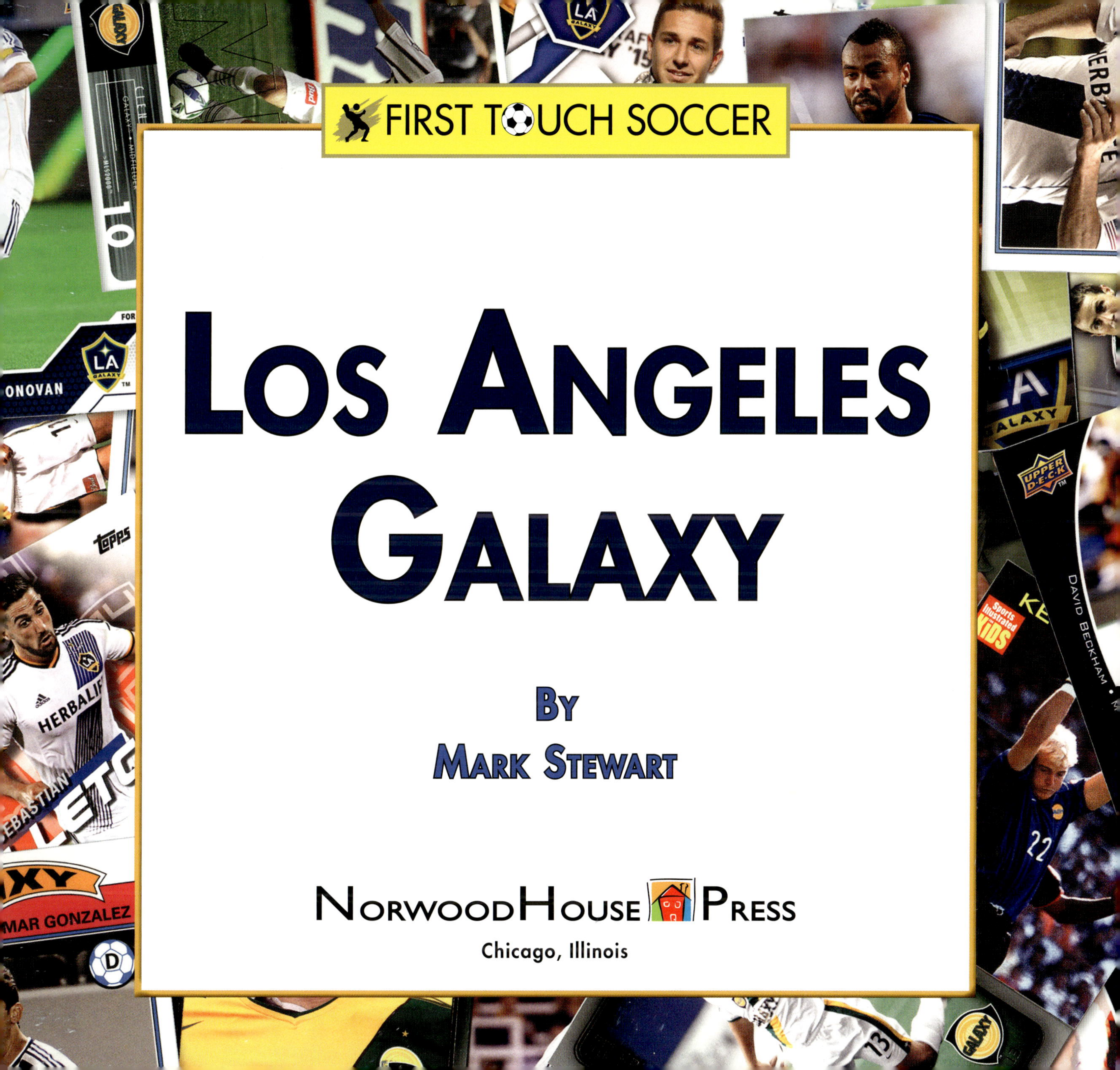

FIRST TOUCH SOCCER

Los Angeles Galaxy

By
Mark Stewart

Norwood House Press
Chicago, Illinois

Norwood House Press

P.O. Box 316598 • Chicago, Illinois 60631
For more information about Norwood House Press please visit our website at www.norwoodhousepress.com or call 866-565-2900.

Photography and Collectibles:
The trading cards and other memorabilia assembled in the background for this book's cover and interior pages are all part of the author's collection and are reproduced for educational and artistic purposes.

All photos courtesy of Associated Press except the following individual photos and artifacts (page numbers): The Upper Deck Company LLC (6, 10 both), Sports Illustrated (11 top), Topps, Inc. (11 middle & bottom, 16).

Cover image: Wally Caddow/Associated Press

Designer: Ron Jaffe
Series Editor: Mike Kennedy
Content Consultants: Michael Jacobsen, Ben Gould and Jonathan Wentworth-Ping
Project Management: Black Book Partners, LLC
Editorial Production: Lisa Walsh

Library of Congress Cataloging-in-Publication Data
Names: Stewart, Mark, 1960 July 7- author.
Title: Los Angeles Galaxy / By Mark Stewart.
Description: Chicago Illinois : Norwood House Press, 2017. | Series: First Touch Soccer | Includes bibliographical references and index. | Audience: Age 5-8. | Audience: K to Grade 3.
Identifiers: LCCN 2016058202 (print) | LCCN 2017005787 (ebook) | ISBN 9781599538648 (library edition : alk. paper) | ISBN 9781684040834 (eBook)
Subjects: LCSH: Los Angeles Galaxy (Soccer team)--History--Juvenile literature.
Classification: LCC GV943.6.L68 S74 2017 (print) | LCC GV943.6.L68 (ebook) | DDC 796.334/640979494--dc23
LC record available at https://lccn.loc.gov/2016058202

302N--072017
Manufactured in the United States of America in North Mankato, Minnesota.

Contents

Words in **bold type** are defined on page 24.

In soccer, star players often go by a one-word nickname. In this book, we use the nickname followed by the player's (*full name*).

Robbie Keane and Landon Donovan—two of the world's top players—celebrate after winning the 2012 Major League Soccer championship game.

MEET THE GALAXY

Los Angeles has been home to championship soccer teams for more than 60 years. Californians from many different backgrounds played in the city long before that. Now the game is part of everyday life.

The Los Angeles Galaxy have taken soccer to a whole new level. The club has put some of the world's best players on the field. They are proud to carry on L.A.'s great soccer tradition.

Time Machine

The Galaxy began play in 1996. They were one of 10 teams that made up Major League Soccer (MLS) that year. The Galaxy played in the **MLS Cup** for the league title three times before they finally won it. In 2014, they became the first club to win the MLS Cup five times. The Galaxy's great players include **Mauricio Cienfuegos**, Cobi Jones, and Carlos Ruiz.

Cobi Jones leads the team cheer after the Galaxy won the CONCACAF championship in 2000. L.A. beat a club from Honduras in the final.

Fans at Galaxy matches can watch from their seats or relax on a grassy bank near the top of the stadium.

BEST SEAT IN THE HOUSE

The Galaxy play their home matches in a stadium built specially for soccer. It is about a half-hour south of Los Angeles, in the city of Carson. The stadium holds 27,000 fans. For many years, the team shared the stadium with another MLS club, Chivas USA. It is one of the best soccer stadiums in the U.S.

COLLECTOR'S CORNER

These collectibles show some of the best Galaxy players ever.

KEVIN HARTMAN

Goalkeeper

1997–2006

Hartman made more saves than anyone in MLS history. In 2003, he set a record with 12 saves in one match.

LANDON DONOVAN

Forward

First Year with Club: 2005

Donovan was one of soccer's most exciting stars. He scored his 100th goal for the Galaxy in 2014.

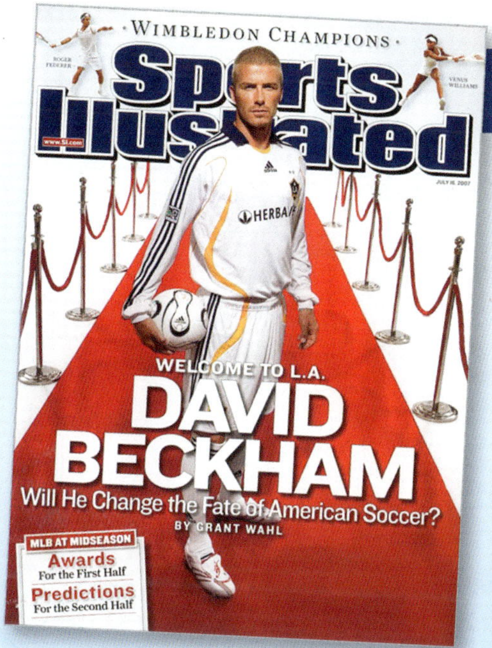

David Beckham

Midfielder

2007–2012

When Beckham decided to play soccer in America, it brought millions of new fans to the game. He was front-page news!

Omar Gonzalez

Defender

2009–2015

Gonzalez was a college star before joining the Galaxy. His great defense helped them win three MLS Cups.

Robbie Keane

Forward

2011–2016

Keane's goal-scoring made the Galaxy one of the top clubs in MLS. He proved to be a good team leader, too.

Worthy Opponents

The sports fans of Southern California don't always see eye-to-eye with the sports fans of Northern California. So it is no surprise that the Galaxy's greatest rivals are the Earthquakes. They play six hours north, in San Jose. It is one of the great rivalries in MLS.

Three players go up for a header in a match between the Earthquakes and Galaxy, but it's Omar Gonzalez who gets there first.

CLUB WAYS

Many fans of the Galaxy have formed special groups. They have names like the Angel City Brigade and Galaxians. They meet before games to tailgate in the parking lot. They sit together in the same sections of the stadium. They wear team colors and special scarves to show their support.

The Angel City Brigade fills the air with blue, gold, and white streamers during a 2011 game.

On the Map

The Galaxy bring together players from many countries. These are some of the best:

1 **Cobi Jones** • Detroit, Michigan

2 **Jorge Campos** • Acapulco, Mexico

3 **Donovan Ricketts** • Montego Bay, Jamaica

4 **Hong Myung-bo** • Seoul, South Korea

5 **Ashley Cole** • London, England

6 **Emmanuel Boateng** • Accra, Ghana

7 **Leonardo (Jose Leonardo Ribeiro da Silva)**
São Paulo, Brazil

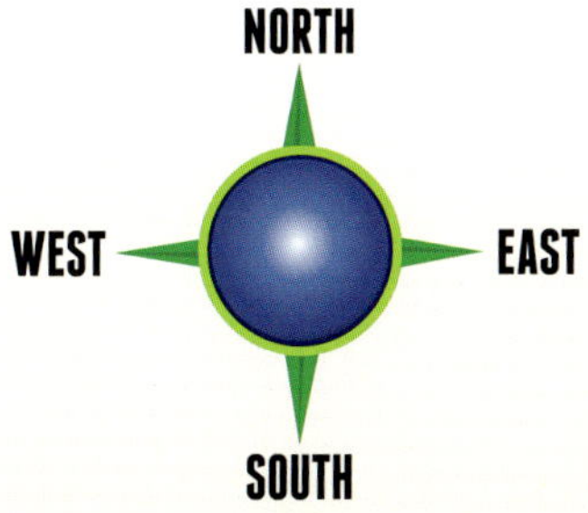

Map of North and Central America

The Galaxy's home stadium is in Carson, California.

World Map

David Beckham shows off the Galaxy's modern uniform, which includes the club crest.

Kit and Crest

When David Beckham joined the Galaxy in 2007, the team switched to white uniforms with touches of blue and gold. Their away **kit** is dark blue. Before Beckham came to Los Angeles, the team wore green and gold. The team's crest shows a quasar. A quasar is created in outer space when galaxies come together.

WE WON!

The MLS Cup is the league's championship game. The Galaxy was the first club to win it five times. Their greatest victory came in 2002. The Galaxy faced the New England Revolution. After 90 minutes, neither team had scored. They played another 23 minutes of **extra time** before Carlos Ruiz found an opening in the defense. He scored the winning goal on a pass from Tyrone Marshall.

The Galaxy players celebrate their 2002 victory. Carlos Ruiz and Cobi Jones hold up the club's championship trophies.

For the Record

The Galaxy have won more than a dozen major tournaments and league championships!

MLS Cup

2002
2005
2011
2012
2014

U.S. Open Cup

2001
2005

Supporters' Shield*

1998
2002
2010
2011

CONCACAF Champions Cup**

2000

* *The Supporters' Shield is awarded to the MLS club with the best record.*

** *The CONCACAF Champions Cup is given to the best team in North America, Central America, and the Caribbean.*

These stars have won major MLS awards while playing for the Galaxy:

1999 Kevin Hartman • Goalkeeper of the Year
1999 Robin Fraser • Defender of the Year
2002 Carlos Ruiz • Most Valuable Player
2002 Carlos Ruiz • MLS Cup MVP
2005 Guillermo Ramirez • MLS Cup MVP
2008 Sean Franklin • Rookie of the Year
2008 Landon Donovan • Golden Boot
2009 Omar Gonzalez • Rookie of the Year
2009 Landon Donovan • Most Valuable Player
2010 Donovan Ricketts • Goalkeeper of the Year
2011 Omar Gonzalez • Defender of the Year
2011 Landon Donovan • MLS Cup MVP
2012 Omar Gonzalez • MLS Cup MVP
2014 Robbie Keane • Most Valuable Player
2014 Robbie Keane • MLS Cup Most Valuable Player

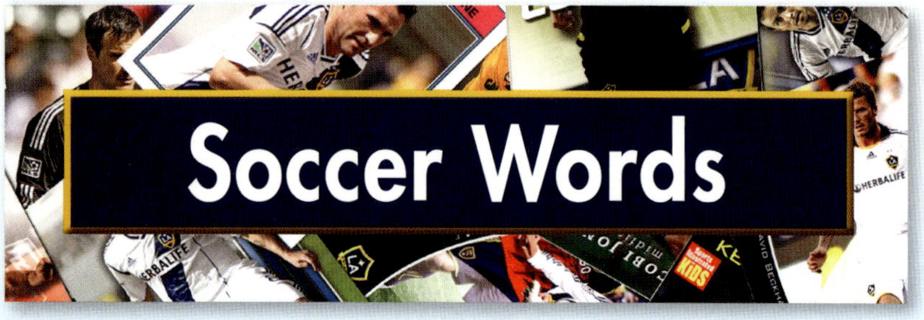

Soccer Words

Extra Time
The 15-minute periods played by MLS clubs when a match is tied after 90 minutes.

Kit
The official league equipment of soccer players, including a club's uniform.

MLS Cup
The championship game of Major League Soccer.

Index

Photos are on **BOLD** numbered pages.

About the Author

Mark Stewart has been writing about world soccer since the 1990s, including *Soccer: A History of the World's Most Popular Game.* In 2005, he co-authored Major League Soccer's 10-year anniversary book.

About the Los Angeles Galaxy

Learn more at these websites:
www.lagalaxy.com
www.MLSsoccer.com
www.teamspiritextras.com